illustrated by **Marc Brown**
story by **Rosemary Wells**

LITTLE, BROWN AND COMPANY
New York · Boston

"Get out the map!" said Papa Gulp.
"Dizzyworld, here we come!" sang Mama Gulp.
"Wow!" shouted Sister Gulp. "Roller Coaster Mania!"
"And deep-fried Devil Dogs!" Brother Gulp chimed in.

"I'd rather sip a carrot shake and go paddling in the duck pond," said little sister Dawn.
Papa revved up the engine, and the American Dreamliner hit the road.

By the time they reached the end of the driveway, the Gulps had
snarfed down all their Winky-Twinks and Jiffy-Chips.
Soon they pulled into a Belly-up Burger.
"We don't even have to get out of the car!" Mama said with delight.

"Four Bloat Burgers with Cheez, please, and Ultrasize those fries!"
said Papa.
"I'll have a salad," said Dawn.

The Dreamliner wheezed and rattled down the road until finally
it sputtered to a stop.
"Flat tire!" said Brother.
"It must be the carburetor again," said Mama.
Only Dawn really knew what was wrong.
"The car says no!" declared Dawn. "This family's too fat to roll!"

"Maybe we should lighten the load," said Papa.
The Gulps chucked out three TVs and a microwave.
But the Dreamliner might as well have been parked in cement.

"I'm hungry!" said Brother. "I wish the pizza man would come!"
"Sometimes just wishing makes things happen!" said Mama.
There was a knock on the door. It was Farmer Spratt.
"Need any help?" he asked.

"A little engine trouble," explained Papa.
"Is there any place to eat around here?" asked Mama.
"My goodness!" said Farmer Spratt. "We've got plenty to eat.
Come and stay for supper! "

The Spratts cooked supper fresh from the garden.
The Gulps watched nervously. None of it was take-out.
None of it was frozen, or came in a can.
"What is it?" whispered Brother.
"It's *green*," whispered Sister.

The Gulps were too polite to say that they didn't ever put anything green into their mouths. They hid the salad in their shirts, and went to bed hungry. Except Dawn, who fell asleep full of sweet corn and zucchini bread.

The next day, there was work to be done on the farm, and the Gulps did their best to help. Papa tried to patch the henhouse roof, but he couldn't get up the ladder.

Mama couldn't reach the eggs on the henhouse floor.
Sister and Brother picked snap beans, but they were too heavy to carry.
Dawn learned to bake Apple Pan Dowdy from scratch.

The next morning the Gulps were so sore they
could hardly move.
"We're not really used to outdoor work," said Mama.
"What do you do at home?" asked Farmer Spratt.
"Mostly watch TV," answered Papa.

"Well, why not come along on our hike down
to the County Fair?" Mrs. Spratt suggested.
"That sounds great!" said Dawn.
"We never walk!" groaned Papa.
"Except to the refrigerator," said Mama.

The County Fair was worth the hike. It had everything.
"Deep-fried corn dogs!" shouted Mama with tears of joy.
"Miles and miles of Funnel Cake!" crowed Papa Gulp.
There was a country music band, a hay wagon ride,
and a Killer Whale Waterslide.

But the dance floor collapsed under two Gulps jitterbugging.
The wheels on the hay wagon snapped off when the Gulps got in.
And four Gulps at once were too much for the waterslide.
They got stuck, and it had to be closed down.

Dawn woke up the family the next morning at 6 a.m.
"If the Dreamliner is ever going to roll again," said Dawn,
"somebody's going to have to exercise and eat right."
"Sometimes wishing makes things happen!" Mama said.
"Mama," replied Dawn, "stop wishing and start working!"

"Soda for breakfast is history, " Dawn declared. "No snacks, candy, or chips. Nothing frozen, fried, or dyed. No heaping helpings. Fresh from the farm only. And lots of outdoor work!"
"We'll starve to death," said Mama.

But the Gulps did not starve.
Bit by bit they got out and got fit.

Bite by bite they began to eat right.

The Gulps
were eating green — and
green tasted
great!

By summer's end, they were stacking hay bales,
mowing and fencing, hoeing and wood chopping,
bucket hauling, and painting the woodshed.

Mama picked up dozens of eggs.
Papa went up the ladder without breaking a single rung.
Brother and Sister carried baskets of beans and tomatoes
with no trouble at all.

"Try the Dreamliner, Pop!" said Dawn one morning.
It started right up and rolled out of its place.
"Get out the map!" whooped Papa.
"Where are you going?" asked the Spratts.

"We're going to climb Mount Dauntless!" said Mama.
The Gulps thanked the Spratts, and everybody kissed good-bye.
Then the Dreamliner headed for the hills.

Soon it was lunchtime.
On one side of the road was a Porker Heaven.
On the other was a Captain Cluck's Chicken.
In front of them was a Belly-up Burger.
"Oh, no! There's nothing to eat!" cried Mama.

"What's that?" asked Dawn suddenly.
"Hot diggity," shouted Brother, "it's a Salad Circus!"
"Six hundred different kinds of salad!" cheered Sister.

Two minutes later the Gulps were inside and ordering.
"Don't forget to Ultrasize those tomatoes!" said Papa.
The Gulps chowed down.
Then the American Dreamliner tore up the highway.
It went sixty-five miles an hour uphill. . .with no trouble at all.

To Beezoo — Rosemary Wells

*For all the kids who love spinach but didn't know it. — Marc Brown*

Text copyright © 2007 by Rosemary Wells · Illustrations copyright © 2007 by Marc Brown · All rights reserved.

Except as permitted under the U.S. Copyright Act of 1976, no part of this publication may be reproduced, distributed, or transmitted in any form or by any means, or stored in a database or retrieval system, without the prior written permission of the publisher.

Little, Brown and Company · Hachette Book Group USA · 1271 Avenue of the Americas, New York, NY 10020

Visit our Web site at www.lb-kids.com · First Edition: April 2007 · 10 9 8 7 6 5 4 3 2 1

Library of Congress Cataloging-in-Publication Data  Wells, Rosemary. The Gulps / Rosemary Wells ; illustrated by Marc Brown.—1st ed.  p. cm.

Summary: After their van and the Killer Whale water slide break down under the strain of their excessive weight, the Gulps decide to eat right and exercise.

ISBN-13: 978-0-316-01460-1  ISBN-10: 0-316-01460-5  [1. Obesity—Fiction. 2. Weight control—Fiction.] I. Brown, Marc Tolon, ill. II. Title.

PZ7.W46843Gul 2007  [E]—dc22  2006026468

SC · Manufactured in China · The paintings in this book were done in gouache on gessoed birch wood.